SPORTY KIDS

LITTLE ATHLETICS

WITHDRAWN

COLLECT ALL THE SPORTY KIDS!

Joe is awesome at footy.
So why is handballing
so hard?

Emma is a swimming
superstar. But can she
learn to dive?

Stefan has winning
racquet skills. But will
he ever play a real
game of tennis?

Abby always wins
at soccer. So why won't
Pete join her team?

Luca never loses on the handball court. But can he beat the school's Handball King?

Jessica is a basketball all-star. So why does she need lucky shoes?

Lizzie loves to talk about netball. So why don't her teammates want to listen?

Pete's family is crazy for cricket. But can he take home the Jacaranda Cup?

FELICE ARENA
ILLUSTRATED BY TOM JELLETT

SPORTY KIDS

LITTLE ATHLETICS

PUFFIN BOOKS

PUFFIN BOOKS

UK | USA | Canada | Ireland | Australia
India | New Zealand | South Africa | China

Penguin Books is part of the Penguin Random House group of companies
whose addresses can be found at global.penguinrandomhouse.com.

Penguin
Random House
Australia

First published by Penguin group (Australia), 2015
This edition published by Penguin Random House Australia Pty Ltd, 2017

1 3 5 7 9 10 8 6 4 2

Design by Tony Palmer © Penguin Group (Australia)
Typeset in 18pt New Century Schoolbook
Colour separation by Splitting Image Colour Studio, Clayton, Victoria
Printed and bound in Australia by Griffin Press,
an accredited ISO AS/NZS 14001
Environmental Management Systems printer.

National Library of Australia Cataloguing-in-Publication data:
Arena, Felice, author.
Sporty kids: Netball/Felice Arena.

ISBN 978 0 14 378318 3

Other Authors/Contributors: Jellett, Tom, illustrator.

penguin.com.au

CHAPTER ONE

Lucy stepped up to the
starting line, ready to race.
This was her favourite
competition in Little
Athletics – the 70-metre
sprint.

Lucy loved to run. And she could go really, really fast. She was so fast that she always won.

But winning wasn't too
hard when she was running
against her friends Emma,
Joe and Stefan.

They were just there to
have fun.

'I'm going to run as fast as a cheetah,' Emma said. 'That's the fastest land animal on earth. *Raaarrr!*'

'It can't beat a machine,' said Joe. 'I'm going to run as fast as an awesome motorbike. *VRRROOOOOM!*'

Stefan laughed. 'Good luck beating me. I'm a running robot with rocket-powered legs.'

Lucy rolled her eyes.

The starter blew the whistle. 'Get into your lanes,' she called. 'On your marks... Set...'

BANG!

And they were off!

CHAPTER TWO

Lucy bolted. She left the cheetah, the motorbike and the running robot far behind.

But at the 40-metre mark, she noticed that

another runner was right
beside her.

It was a new kid – a girl
she had never raced against
before.

The parents on the
sidelines were cheering
loudly.

Lucy willed herself
to run faster than ever.
But she couldn't break
away.

In seconds, the girl was sprinting ahead of her.

This can't be happening, thought Lucy.

Her legs were beginning
to feel heavy and wobbly.
But the finishing line
was only a few metres
away. Keep going, she told

herself. You can do it!

Lucy raced until she was next to the new girl. It was going to be a close finish…

CHAPTER THREE

But the new girl beat Lucy
to the finishing line.

Lucy couldn't believe it.
This was the first time she
had been beaten, and it
didn't feel good. Not one bit.

15

'What an awesome race,'
said Emma. 'I was like
whoooosh! And Joe was like
vrroooom! And Stefan was
like *beep-boop-beep-boop!*

Joe and I came equal
fourth, and Stefan came in
sixth. And you ran second –
which is amazing.'

'But I didn't win,' said
Lucy.

18

She looked over at her dad. He was waving to her from the sidelines.

'You ran even faster than last time!' he said, giving her a huge hug. 'You should be very proud of yourself.'

But Lucy just sighed.

'Come on,' said Joe. 'They're calling us for shot-put. Let's go.'

CHAPTER FOUR

Lucy was determined to win the shot-put. It wasn't her best event, but she usually did pretty well.

'I'm totally going to win this,' she said to Joe.

She picked up the shot
and stepped into the circle.
She tucked the shot beside
her chin, pointed her other
arm out, and threw.

The shot landed with a
thud in the soggy grass.
It was a really good throw.

'5.71 metres,' said the official.

Lucy had broken her own record for the second time that day. And she was in the lead.

Her dad gave her a thumbs up.

Emma and Joe ran over to congratulate her.

Stefan stepped up to the
circle.

Lucy could tell he was
pretending to be a cannon
on a pirate ship. Every
time he threw the shot he'd
shout, '*KABOOM!*'

The only one left was the new kid.

'OOOOOMPH!' she grunted as she threw the shot.

'5.75 metres,' said the official.

Lucy couldn't believe it. The new girl was in first place again!

The long jump was the last
event of the day, and Lucy
was focussed on winning it.

When it was the new
girl's turn, she bolted down
the run-up track and took a
huge leap forward.

Lucy could tell it was an awesome leap, even before the new girl landed in the sand.

It was the longest jump of the day.

'I'll have to jump the longest I've ever jumped,' she said to Stefan as she waited to take her run up. 'I've got to beat that new kid.'

'Charlotte!' said Stefan.

'What?' Lucy asked.

'The new kid. Her name's Charlotte,' Stefan said. 'I talked to her after the shot-put. She's just moved here from another state.'

Lucy wished that
Charlotte had stayed there.

Lucy sprinted down the
runway and timed her run
perfectly.

Her front right foot hit
the centre of the take-off

board, and she launched

herself into the air.

SWOOOOOOSH!

She landed in the sand pit, kicking up sand around her.

It felt like a good jump. She looked up at the official. Had she beat Charlotte? Had she won?

'3.40 metres!' said the official.

Lucy felt like crying. She'd come second again.

'Cheer up,' said Joe. 'You beat your own record three times today. And Charlotte is taller than you. I never ever win but I love Little Athletics.'

Lucy nodded, but she still
felt terrible.

Then she heard the music
of an ice-cream van...

CHAPTER FIVE

Other kids had heard the
music, too. Lots of them were
running towards the van.

'Hey, Dad – catch!' Lucy
called out. She threw her
sports bag towards him.

The bag flew even further than Lucy's shot-put throw! But she was already racing.

She bolted across the oval. There were long lines of witches hats on the sidelines.

Without thinking she took an awesome leap and cleared them.

Lucy shot through the main gates of the athletics field.

She ran along the footpath.

She could see
the giant colourful
pictures of delicious
ice-cream painted
on the side of the van.

Finally the van
stopped on the side
of the road.

Lucy was out in front.
But then she heard
someone running close
behind her.

She glanced back. 'NO
WAY!' she said.

It was Charlotte!

She's not going beat me this time, Lucy thought. She picked up speed.

She was running faster than she had ever run.

Within seconds she had reached the ice-cream truck. She was first in line!

Lucy shot her arms up in the air. She felt as if she had won an Olympic gold medal.

Then she remembered
what it was like to come
second. Charlotte was going
to be miserable!

Lucy turned around to
see if she was okay.

CHAPTER SIX

But Charlotte was grinning.
She didn't look upset at all.

'You're an awesome
runner,' she said. 'How cool
is Little Athletics?'

Lucy was surprised.
'Aren't you mad that you
lost?' she said.

Charlotte shrugged.

'No,' she said. 'I just love running. And I love Little Athletics. But, don't tell anyone – the starter pistol freaks me out sometimes.'

'No way!' said Lucy. 'It freaks me out too!'

'Do you want to hang out together next week after we race?' asked Charlotte.

For the first time that day, Lucy smiled.

She didn't even care that
other kids were buying
their ice-creams first.

'That would be awesome,'
she said.

'What would you like,
girls?' asked the ice-cream
man.

57

'Oh, no!' said Lucy.
'I forgot to get money from
my dad.'

'I forgot too,' said
Charlotte. 'I'm going back...
Want to race?'

'You bet!' Lucy grinned.

'On your marks… Set…GO!'

READ THE BOOKS AND MEET THE SPORTY KIDS...

Abby Walsh

Abby loves to win, especially at soccer. It's her favourite sport and she's the star of the team. She's got the skills to take on anyone!

Angus is fast, clever and knows everything there is to know about Aussie Rules. He's awesome in attack – the footy team's top goal-scorer.

Angus Chung

Ben Jakande

Ben is a fan of everything sporty. He knows all the players, all the stats and every sporting record there is. He's a walking, talking wikipedia of sport!

Emma is creative and loves acting almost as much as sport. She's a great all-rounder with an original way of looking at every sporting situation.

Emma Ashworth

62

Jacqui can tell you who to play in what position, and which tactics to use – she's the brains behind any team. Need a winning strategy? Ask Jacqui!

Jacqui Abraham

Jessica Ito

Jessica is the smallest in the class, but she's also the star of the basketball team. She won't brag about it, though – she thinks she's just very very lucky!

Joe Meyer

Joe is funny, cheeky and loves team sports. He's a terrific all-rounder and a natural at almost everything, so he's keen to give anything a try.

Lizzie is the heart of any team. She's the commentator, scorer and cheer squad, all rolled into one. No one loves sport more than Lizzie!

Lizzie Passad

Luca is super strong
and super confident,
like his twin sister,
Sofia. He's a
natural leader and
the king of the
handball courts
at lunch.

Luca Farelli

Lucy Ko

Lucy is the fastest
kid in class. She's
not so keen on
playing team
sports – but she's
super fit and
the queen of the
athletics track.

Oliver is bigger and stronger than anyone else in class. His favourite sport is swimming. He's not so good at losing – but that's because he usually wins!

Oliver Petersson

Pete Karim

Pete is the ultimate team player, but he also loves to win. He knows how to bring a team together to get the best out of everyone.

Sofia is lots of fun and is super competitive, like her twin brother, Luca. She's awesome at sport, especially ball sports, and she's always the first picked for any team.

Stefan is imaginative and very independent so he loves individual sports like tennis. Give him a sporting skill to learn and he's all over it!

CHARLOTTE'S TIPS ON HOW TO THROW A SHOT!

Not everyone wants to be an Olympic champion, some kids just like to have fun.

Lucy really wants to win and it's great to be competitive, but sometimes when you're relaxed and enjoying yourself, you can achieve even more.

My favourite track and field events are running, long jump and shot-put.

The heavy ball in shot-put is called a shot.

Here's how to throw like an Olympian:

- Hold the shot at the base of your fingers, not in your palm. Bend your hand backwards with your fingers slightly apart.
- Place the shot into your neck, and point your palm in the direction you'll be throwing.
- Step back and bend your knees and hips.
- Push the shot up and away from you.

Other track and field events include discus, hurdles and triple jump. So get out there and have some fun at Little Athletics!

LUCY'S FAVOURITE ATHLETICS JOKES!

What type of shoes are made from
banana skins?
Slippers!

Did you hear about the race
between the lettuce and the tomato?
*The lettuce was a head and the
tomato was trying to ketchup.*

What did the long jump say to
the high jump?
Hi, Jump!

Two waves had a race. Who won?
They tide!

Why was the girl called Saturn so good at athletics?
She could run rings around everyone.

Knock, Knock.
Who's there?
Dozen.
Dozen who?
Dozen anybody want to race?

What is a runner's favourite subject in school?
Jog-raphy!

How do athletes stay cool?
They stand near the fans.

LUCY'S AWESOME ATHLETICS FACTS!

Did you know?

- Around 100,000 kids compete all across Australia every weekend in Little Athletics.
- The first track and field events were staged in Greece at the first Olympics in 776BC.
- The stick that runners hand to each other in a relay is called a baton.
- Australia has produced many world champion athletes, including Ron Clarke, Betty Cuthbert, Robert De Castella, Herb Elliot, Cathy Freeman and Shirley Strickland.

- Usain Bolt is the fastest person on earth. He holds the world record for the 100-metre and 200-metre sprint
- The decathlon is an event that combines ten track and field events – four running events, three throwing events and three jumping events.
- To compete in the triple jump event you need to know how to hop, step and jump.
- The marathon is a long-distance event – marathon runners run for 42 kilometres.
- A starting block is the piece of equipment used by sprint athletes to hold their feet at the start of a race.

FELICE SAYS...
When I was a kid I used
to love jumping over
a narrow creek on my
grandfather's farm.
I did it so many times I
didn't even have to think
about it. But one day it had rained
and I slipped over during take-off.
SPLASH! I landed on my butt on
a giant trout! Yep, long jump is my
favourite athletics event, but it's
also my preferred way of fishing.

TOM SAYS...
At school, sports day was
the day you got to try your
hand at athletics. My best
event was the long jump.
I think my school house
was Buffalo (blue). I could
never really get the hop
skip and a jump bit in the
right order, but as long as the jump
bit was last, you would do okay.